MW01087793

Also by Goran Simić

*Immigrant Blues*
Brick Books, 2003

*from* SARAJEVO, *with* SORROW

*Goran Simic´ crosses the Mitjacka River
on a water run.*

GORAN SIMIĆ

# *from* SARAJEVO *with* SORROW

POEMS

*translations by*
AMELA SIMIĆ

BIBLIOASIS

FIRST EDITION

*Library and Archives Canada Cataloguing in Publication*

Goran, Simić, 1952–
From Sarajevo, with sorrow: poems / Goran Simić;
translations by Amela Simić.

ISBN 0-9735971-6-X (LIMITED ED, CASED)
ISBN 0-9735971-5-1 (PBK.)

1.   Sarajevo (Bosnia and Herzegovina)
—History—1992–1996—Poetry.
I.   Simić, Amela   II.   Title.
PS8587.I3119F76 2005      C891.8'21      C2005-902167-5


EDITED BY
Salvatore Ala & Daniel Wells


PRINTED AND BOUND IN CANADA

# CONTENTS

# PREFACE

## I. GHOST BOOK OF HORROR

For whom were these poems intended at the time I wrote them, during the shameless Bosnian war and the siege of Sarajevo? For whom were these poems written under candlelight, between 1992 and 1995?

To be sure, not for those who roamed with me all over the city with empty canisters in hand looking for fresh running water. The water supplied by the UN soldiers who came to Sarajevo to keep four hundred thousand of us alive was bitter and smelled of chlorine. When the UN left there were eleven thousand new graves. These poems are not for those of us who were clay pigeons waiting in a long line for the humanitarian aid and food which came from all over the world. It was bitter food, because it was served as a poor excuse. Everybody now knows the way these countries compensated for their dirty consciences by feeding our walking dead, while they did nothing to stop the siege.

I did not write these poems for those of us who stayed with our children in order to prove that Sarajevo, with its mix of different people of various nationalities and backgrounds, did not differ from any other city in the world. We lived in peace for a very long time without anybody's help.

11

I did not write them for those who filled the new graveyards in converted soccer fields, for my mother and my brother who are buried there, nor for my family house which now looks like an ashtray. Nor for my bookshop, which was so thoroughly and repeatedly looted it does not exist anymore. So, for whom? The answer is still not clear to me, ten years later, living in the heart of Toronto. There are so many questions I still ask myself.

The lines I wrote were written in the belief that, when compared with the cold newspaper reports which would be forgotten with the start of a new war elsewhere, only poetry could be a true and decent witness to war. I remain uncertain whether this is because the history of horror is a bad teacher or we are bad pupils. I simply wrote what I saw. Perhaps I wrote them to explain to myself the fear in my children's eyes when they walked along streets covered in blood. Or to comfort myself with the fact that I went to so many funerals, but nobody went to mine. New wars have indeed replaced old wars, and it is hard to believe that ten years have passed since my own war ended, ten years since I wrote these poems as a poet, a witness and a survivor.

I also wrote these poems for myself, once an established poet ready to pack his suitcase and be a poet again, but now with a strange accent and an even stranger past. I have joined the ranks of those poets who have lost their own tribal language and country, and then gone on to a place where the weight of previously published books is worth almost nothing.

As a human being, I wish I'd never experienced the horror that I went through. That's what my nightmares often tell me, as does my strange need to hide every time I hear firecrackers that sound the same as exploding grenades. But as a poet, I would be deeply sorry if I hadn't stayed, in the middle of horror, a witness to how cheap life can be. As cheap in war-torn Bosnia, in the heart of Europe, as it is in Rwanda, in the middle of Africa. So I am a divided person. But my reader will not recognize this.

These poems are a cry for those who will never read them, a testimony to the absurdity of war, and a bridge that connects innocent victims and those responsible for the crimes, so that they can recognize themselves between the lines.

In Sarajevo hell I wrote these poems as epitaph and testimony. I needed to be alive through poetry. It just so happened that, during the siege, a Bosnian daily newspaper twice published my name by mistake in the list of people killed in the first year of the war. For another three years I wondered why people looked at me so strangely. I was already a ghost, but I did not know it.

## II. DRESSING UP THE GHOST

THE WORST THING that can happen to a poet is to lose not a manuscript, but an already published book. This is what happened to me when *Sarajevo Sorrow* was published in the middle of the siege. I had readers who wanted others to read my book even more than they themselves needed to read my testimony. And so, this book became a phantom book.

It circulated all over Europe while I was living in Sarajevo without any contact with the world outside of Bosnia. The book began living its own life. Without me. It was mostly used to freshen the air. Some publishers used it for political purposes; some published it

13

for profit, while still others used it for humanitarian causes. Living in a besieged city, I lost all control of my own poetry. By pure accident, I received single copies of my book translated and published in other languages. I got a copy from Slovenia, from two different publishers in Serbia, from Poland. Somebody told me that it was also published in France, and some friends even printed it in Canada as a chapbook.

The only recognition I received as a living author came from Denmark, Finland, Norway and Sweden, thanks to friends who managed to get my poetry manuscript out of Bosnia. At that time Bosnia was treated as a huge septic hole and I am not surprised that UN soldiers were told not to let out of the Sarajevo walls the kind of writing which could stink up the rest of Europe. I call it occupation by double censors: by people who tried to prove that writing may be painful even when it doesn't stink. Obviously they didn't think of art as a bridge.

The greatest publicity many of these poems received occurred after fellow poet David Harsent published them in England under the title *Sprinting from the Graveyard* (Oxford University Press, 1997). But David, to whom I owe appreciation for the friendship he extended when siege and horror were my cruel realities, defined his editing of my poetry as his own version. Not being familiar with English, and especially not with the copyright law, I didn't realize the weight of the definition of "version" until recently. Instead of talking to me as the author, my publisher was redirected to negotiate the re-publishing of my own poetry with an agent who represented the author of this "version," since he was also the sole holder of copyright.

14

I became a ghost again. My poems, originally published in translation by my ex-wife Amela Simić, became a ghost book. I found myself sitting next to a fire with a melting snowball in my hand. To make a long story short, the price to get my "versioned" poetry back was too high. Biblioasis, Amela and I decided to re-translate the poems, and publish them in a version much closer in form and language to the originals. If nothing else, we hoped to give this ghost poetry a shape. The only difference is that I've added some of my unpublished poems, written in Sarajevo during the siege, which I have translated into English myself.

I know who to thank at the end of this strange journey. But privately, I think I should give thanks to the poetry which has come back to me. I guess.

*from* SARAJEVO

After I buried my mother, running from the
shelling of the graveyard; after soldiers returned
my brother's body wrapped in a tarp; after I saw
the fire reflected in the eyes of my children as
they ran to the cellar among the dreadful rats;
after I wiped with a dishtowel the blood from
the face of an old woman, fearing I would
recognize her; after I saw a hungry dog licking
the blood of a man lying at a crossing: after
everything, I would like to write poems which
resemble newspaper reports, so bare and cold
that I could forget them the very moment a
stranger asks: Why do you write poems which
resemble newspaper reports?

## THE FACE OF SORROW

I have seen the face of sorrow. It is the face of
the Sarajevo wind leafing through newspapers
glued to the street by a puddle of blood as I
pass with a loaf of bread under my arm.

As I run across the bridge, full water canisters
in hand, it is the face of the river carrying the
corpse of a woman on whose wrist I notice
a watch.

I saw that face again in the gesture of a hand
shoving a child's shoe into a December furnace.

It is the face I find in inscriptions on the back of
family photographs fallen from a garbage truck.

It is the face which resists the pencil, incapable of
inventing the vocabulary of sorrow, the face with
which I wake to watch my neighbour standing
by the window, night after night, staring into
the dark.

CHRISTMAS TREE DECORATIONS

My children and I decorate the Christmas tree.
Outside the moon howls in the eyes of a hungry dog.
I have brought from the attic a box of family ornaments.
We recognize in their reflections
our own joyful faces from past years.

The shining decoration on top is my Grandfather.
From the Russian war he brought home
just the bullet in his shoulder,
and the need not to speak
whenever conversation turned to war.
Why did he die with a smile on his face?

This other ornament is my Uncle's,
a war hero who jumped from his hospital window.
The doctors said he often dreamt
of bombs being thrown into his room.
When he died he had so shriveled
we buried him in a child's coffin,
too small to display all his medals.

That next decoration is of another Uncle.
He was convinced that Communists
had planted a bug in his mouth,
which was why he spoke a language
of his own invention.
He died in prison after authorities discovered
his strange words sounded like secret codes.

The next bauble belongs to my Aunt.
While gathering wildflowers
with which to decorate the liberators,
she didn't notice that she had wandered into a minefield,
and never found out her husband
was not among them.

Perhaps he would have been,
if only he'd not been so fond of dancing
to the grenades clinking round his waist.

The red decoration is my Father.
At the end of the war he came home a hero,
but amid the celebrations scattered the brains
of a drunk comrade who'd tried to rape a village girl.
He'd still be in prison
if that girl hadn't been his sister.
He remained imprisoned long after his release.

This decoration, here, is my Brother.
He never learned to properly fire a rifle.
The last time he pulled the trigger
he shot a Christmas tree and died of sorrow.

This last small black ornament is Mother.
After surviving the concentration camp
she dedicated her life to lighting candles,
and washing family graves.

I stand with my children
at the foot of the Christmas tree.
There are no more decorations.
I am thinking about how nicely
the tree's trunk will burn in our stove,
as my children dream of the morning
and the presents that await them.

*Tomorrow we will wake up happy.*
*Tomorrow we will wake up happy.*

## THE WALL OF HORROR

I've heard the March leaf of the calendar
belonging to the girl next door fall. For hours
she looks at her big stomach as at a wall behind
which moves a being nailed to her womb by
drunk soldiers in a camp on the other side of the
river. She stares at the wall of horror behind
which a disease begins, a terrible disease which
lives on images and silence. Perhaps she sees her
maiden dress fluttering on a pole like a flag.
Perhaps she feels the steps of the murderer in the
sound of the falling leaf, the one she will
recognize when the child starts to resemble
something she will try to forget all her life. I
don't know. All I heard was the March leaf of the
calendar fall.

# THE BRIDGE

On the eve of war, a foreign film crew appeared
in Rŭza's village and turned her country idyll
into chaos: prefabricated shacks were assembled
and quickly painted; the skilled foreigners even
built a bridge in half a day, while embarrassed
local craftsmen looked on. The greediest
villagers became part of the history of the village
through a camera lens, taking the parts of Indians
in the Western screenplay. Pierced by arrows,
they fell from trees; shot by Winchester rifles,
they rolled down steep hills. They jumped into
rivers, fleeing cowboys, and at night they would
heal their bruises with Bosnian brandy and herbs.
One evening, the film workers took the set apart
and disappeared into the night, leaving behind
only the bridge which nobody crossed for a
long time.

I watch Rŭza writing a letter to her brother
who lives across that river where corpses float
like shadows. Bent over the letter, she resembles
the bridge, and even the collapsed wall of her
house looks like a film set. And I see her
covering that scar on her neck, left long ago by
some film extra who carelessly handled his bow
and arrow.

# CITY AND DOGS

At the beginning of the war the city streets resembled a catwalk of the most beautiful dogs. Their masters had mercilessly left them when fleeing the burning city. Only the smell of petrol and the dogs' eyes full of horror remained. After losing their battle with some strays on the trash heaps, these abandoned dogs withdrew to the doorways of their locked apartments and died honourably, barking every time a shell whistled.

Once, looking for a sniper, we broke down the door of an abandoned apartment and found the skeleton of an old woman who had merged with her kitchen chair. For a long time we debated the religion of the old woman who had starved to death, despite a pantry full of canned food.

Neither the photographs littering her apartment, nor the unfinished Gobelin of a knight in front of his castle, nor the hundreds of perfume bottles revealed the secret of her piously folded hands.

When we carried her out, lighter than our army bags, it was already dawn. A pack of hungry dogs was fighting on the trash heap. Someone remarked that God would have his hands full after this war, and we were silent, pretending not to notice the can opener flickering on the chain around the neck of the skeleton of this old lady who had once belonged to a rich family.

## A COMMON STORY

Seeing off his wife and children, who were
fleeing Sarajevo in January of 1993, my friend
wrote on the frozen bus window: "I am with
you." He never wrote anything else. I signed his
army card. I wrote his pleas to leave the city.
I wrote appeals for this man whose words were
washed away by an unknown bus washer. Later, I
wrote long and tender letters to his wife, and
kissed his children a hundred times.

When they brought him to the hospital, half his
body missing, I ran to read him that first letter
from his wife, a letter full of tenderness I had
composed quickly. He did not hear it. He was
fighting for breath and only I knew that he was
fighting for those words, "I am with you,"
washed into the sewer long ago by a bus washer.

## A NEWSPAPER REPORT ON PARCELS

When the war broke out, I believed that all
good people had stayed in the penitentiary
Sarajevo had become, and I secretly missed my
friends, who did not have enough nerve for this
theatre of death.

Then the first parcels from my brother arrived,
and on the lacquered surface of the kitchen table,
I saw my mother with a can opener in her hands.
Later, when the parcels of flour from friends
arrived, their letters hurt me more than the sight
of the dying town. I looked at the bottom of the
parcels as at a border beyond which I believed
that many good people moved into the world
of letters.

The very morning the first parcel of hunger
arrived, my mother caressed me with her floury
hands, and then vanished into the kitchen sink.
And I still look at my reflection in the smooth
surface of the kitchen table, and ask myself what
I have asked myself a thousand times: have only
the good and brave people stayed in Sarajevo, in
this city where one must not whistle because it
resembles the sound of shells? Where my wife
looks at the blocked kitchen sink every day, and
doesn't understand why I won't clean it?

# RŮZA AND THE TRAMS

All that Růza left behind was her weasel-fur
collar and her monthly public transit pass. The
trams were junk heaps long ago. Růza is already
used to soft heaven, and takes long walks with
the angels. She does not need the pass anymore.
Among the shadows in her wardrobe, the only
thing real is a conductor's greasy fingerprint on
her monthly pass.

Is he still alive? Will his fingers ever touch
Růza's fur collar again? I don't know, I don't
know. Honest to God, I don't know how to
think after a year of war.

# WAR MICE

In the second summer of the war the town was overrun by rats. At night they crept out of the sewer and occupied the empires of the trash heap. They would sometimes attack cats and even lost children, and at first dark we locked our doors. Yet as though by some secret agreement, our apartments were invaded by mice. We discovered them in our flour supply, among our Sunday clothes, and the more we exterminated the more there were. The first mouse caught in a mousetrap behind the piano we called "the artist." Later the nameless swarms of mice we trapped and killed had only numbers.

None but I even remembers the first victim who died in this city, followed by the black statistics of Sarajevo's dead. *What was her name?* I try to remember and I bring down from the attic a box of obituary notices. But I find inside only shredded paper and the frightened eyes of the mice nation, which we have been unable to destroy for centuries. They also do not know the name of their first victim, nor the name of the country they left long ago.

## MEDALS

When he returned from the war my grandfather
locked himself in the attic and did not come out
for fifteen days. During the day he was silent, but
at night he would moan so terribly that the
candles burning under the icon went out. When
he finally came downstairs, my grandmother saw
the face of death.

When my father returned from the war in his
blood-stained coat, he spilled a heap of medals
from his bag and went up to the attic without
looking at anyone. During the day we compared
his medals with grandfather's, and at night we
buried our heads under the pillows so as not to
hear him moaning and calling out to his dead
friends. Come morning, my mother would put
his shiny medals on the window sill for
passers-by to see. But no one passed our house
anymore because no one could bear the
moaning. One morning we found a ghost in the
coat by the bed. The ghost had my father's eyes.

It happened a long time ago. The family vault
has thickened. The medals still hang on the walls
and officials sometimes take them away during
holidays and bring them back after they are
finished with them. I wouldn't have cared if they
were never returned. Only sometimes after news
of the war, horrified, I notice them on the wall.
Because the only thing left from my father and
my grandfather are those screams and moans, and
I console myself that it is the wind scratching the
dilapidated attic and beams of our simple house.

## THE APPRENTICE

I have spent half my life searching for a
vocabulary of beauty which will exceed the
strange love of paper and pencil. I've acquired
knowledge from shadows, I've learned from
monuments, I've associated with ghosts.

These days I spend more time at funerals than
at my desk, and I notice how the covers of my
book of fairy tales burn on the frozen stove,
warming tea for my sick child. And how beauty
returns to his ruddy cheeks through the dried
linden flower I never thought could be more
beautiful than a rose.

LAMENT FOR VIJECNICA

When the National Library burned for three
days in August, the town was choked with black
snow. Those days I could not find a single pencil
in the house, and when I finally found one it did
not have the heart to write. Even the erasers left
behind a black trace. Sadly, my homeland burned.

Liberated, the heroes of novels wandered around
the city mingling with passers-by and the souls
of dead soldiers. I saw Werther sitting on a
collapsed graveyard fence, Quasimodo swinging
from a mosque's minaret. I heard Raskolnikov
and Mersault whispering in the cellar for days.
Gavroche was in camouflage, and Yossarian had
already traded secrets with the enemy. Not to
mention young Sawyer, who threw himself from
Princip's Bridge into the river for pocket money.

For three days I lived in this ghostly town with
the terrible suspicion that there were fewer and
fewer of us alive, and that the shells fell only for
me. I locked myself in the house and leafed
through tourist guides. I went out only on the
day the radio announced that ten tonnes of coal
had been taken from the library cellar. Only then
did my pencil regain its heart.

## IMAGINATION LOST

God, my imagination is wearing out. My fervour
is fading and acid is eating me up, day after day.
Old blunders replace still older ones, just as last
year's parasols get marked by the same wind with
the initials of the north.

Someone is coming out of nowhere again, and
I begin to remember the summers only by my
dirty tan. God, the silence which flatters my
voice is growing, and I resemble my reflection
in the mirror more and more.

I still walk through walls, but I wake up with
bruises; when my fingers reach for the sky, under
my fingernails I discover mud; when I wish I
were there I leave quickly, but my return lasts
longer because I've run out of questions.

My imagination is wearing out, and I no longer
see my reflection in the eyes of fish as I dive
towards the thing promised me, though I no
longer know what it is. God, Your order of
things puzzles me more and more, because I
see myself standing in the same line I've been in
a thousand times.

And I can see Your bewilderment as You
shorten my walking stick and stare at me, asking
Yourself: how is it he has so many answers to a
question I haven't even considered? And I see
You with a handsaw over Your shoulder as You
leave for the forest, despising the man whose
imagination is vanishing like hoarfrost from a
tree You are approaching. My God.

## WHAT I SAW

I saw that human feet shrink two sizes when a person dies. On the streets of Sarajevo you could see so many shoes in pools of blood. Every time I went out I tied my shoelaces so tight my feet turned blue. God, how happy I was to return home with shoes on my feet. What a pleasure to untie the laces. What a pleasure not to lie on the street without the shoes on my feet.

Before I left the house my mother would check to see if I was wearing clean underwear. She claimed that it would be a shame if they carried me to a mortuary and found dirty underclothes on me. Better to go to a blue sky with blue feet than with no shoes.

What a shame for our family, she'd say. To be killed without dignity. God forbid!

## LOVE STORY

The story of Bosko and Amira was a major media event that Spring. They tried to cross the bridge out of Sarajevo, believing their future was on the other side, where the bloody past had already gone. Death caught them, in the middle of the bridge. The one who pulled the trigger wore a uniform and was never called a murderer.

Newspapers from around the world wrote about them. Italian dailies published stories about the Bosnian Romeo and Juliet. French journalists wrote about a romantic love which surpassed political boundaries. Americans saw in them the symbol of two nations on a divided bridge. And the British illustrated the absurdity of war with their bodies. Only the Russians were silent. Then the photographs of the dead lovers moved into peaceful Springs.

My friend Prsíc, a Bosnian soldier who guarded the bridge, watched each day as maggots, flies, and crows finished off their swollen bodies.

I can still hear his swearing as he put on his gas mask, when the Spring winds from the other side of the bridge brought with it their bodies' stench. No newspapers wrote about that.

## LEJLA'S SECRET

Doctor Lejla, from the Department for Corpse Identification, went mad before the new year. She left the mortuary, scattered all their documents on the street, and locked herself in her apartment with those images of slaughtered bodies, carved ears, and eyeless heads. She responded with screams to every voice on the staircase, and at night she played her out-of-tune piano and howled like a wounded animal.

What was it she saw at the mortuary that day? Like contagion that question began to obsess her neighbours, and the secret of Lejla's madness became our nightmare. Her ghost turned our basement shelter into a workshop of horror. Some believed that she'd recognized the face of her late husband, others that she had seen a corpse sewn from the bodies of different people. The rest saw a baby in an open womb. Before long, fear of our imagination surpassed our fear of the shells. The building was soon deserted.

When they carried her away, wrists cut, on the first day of the new year, nobody came to see her off. Refugees now live in her apartment and sleep peacefully. Only the Devil still wakes to the sound of Lejla's piano.

## OLD PEOPLE AND THE SNOW

My beautiful old ones are disappearing slowly. They simply leave,
without rules, without a farewell.
They stoop down to reach a clothes-peg
and turn into earth.
Just for a day, their names
invade a modest space in the morning paper
and then withdraw before news of the war.
They leave behind their diaries, their letters, and new suits
readied for their funerals long ago. They pass
like a breeze through the curtains of an abandoned apartment.
And we forget their names.
Like that of the retired captain from the ground floor
we spent half the day burying because the graveyard
was shelled so heavily we had to hide in his grave.
For three years, he wrote letters to an imaginary son
and piled them in a shoebox.
Like that of a former employee of a former bank
whose diaries I bought from some refugee children just before
they started to make paper airplanes.
They were written in invisible ink.
Like that of my neighbour whose whole family had been
        massacred in his village,
who had given me the battery radio
he always had with him
before we carried him out of the basement.
He had never bought batteries or tried to switch it on.
It is snowing outside. Just like last year.

Surrounded by keepsakes whose meanings left with the old people,
I try to decipher sorrow's secret handwriting, that message which
        allows a
snowman to watch
a sunrise with indifference.
Or have I already deciphered the message?

Why else would I have forgotten
to switch on the radio at a time when the news from the front
threathened to overpower my need
for letters to nobody, and diaries in which nothing is written?
While it is snowing outside. Just like last year.

## BEŠO'S STORY

After working for a year in the Australian forest, Bešo was sick of it all. He was sick of the smoke pump used to smoke out the venomous snakes, leaving the sugar cane fields safe for the cane-cutters to work. And he was sick of the natives who sold their daughters for shirt buttons. "The day you stopped carrying the anti-venom serum, you became their amulet. Only a man of God would not balk at those first seconds after a snake bite," the manager told him, not noticing as they parted that Bešo trembled.

For a year Bešo poached on the river Darling, hauling dead crocodiles shot by a Czech sniper into a rubber boat. Only when police chased them away did Bešo realize that his own gun didn't have a firing pin. "A second shot could have given us away," said the Czech, "and you would not have stood a chance with a wounded croc." He didn't notice the cigarette quivering in the corner of Bešo's mouth.

Not until the shell whizzed through his apartment and exploded in a neighbouring yard did Bešo ever descend to our cellar colony. "Hurry up, Bešo," I shouted, running downstairs. He just grinned as though he'd heard a good joke. He even came down without noticing he'd walked through his neighbour's blood, whose body we had just taken away. Someone should tell Bešo that the war has lasted for a whole year now.

## SUSAN AND THE DOORFRAME

At the time all of us emaciated prisoners of war looked more like the ghosts of those we'd already buried, Susan Sontag appeared at my door. She stood in my doorway and that little photograph from the cover of her book I was reading grew as big as my door. After that, muddy and wet from rain, she fell asleep on my sofa, and only then did I understand she wasn't a ghost.

When she woke up, she told me how she had once visited the mother of her son's friend, and after she'd rung the bell, Lauren Bacall opened the door. She told me that at that moment the movie screen with Lauren's face became as small as the doorframe.

When she left, she borrowed my travel bag. When she came back the following year, my bag was covered with labels from the biggest airports from around the world. It looked like the whole world had signed my little travel bag. At the same time I was learning how one sniper bullet can penetrate two heads. But I still haven't learned anything about the difference between big and small pictures. When we stand in the doorway we are so big. Yet one's whole life can fit into one small travel bag.

## A STEP TO MADNESS

After three years of war
my neighbour suddenly went mad.
I must not say for no reason at all,
because our judgement was so disturbed
that we even called this slaughterhouse a town.
Once,
when from the top of the poplar across from the Presidential Palace
he cursed the State, the Government, the Army, the Police and God,
he turned to us astonished spectators:
"Why are you staring at me?
You'll do the same tomorrow."

It was the most precise formulation of fear,
a fear which had been gathering under our skins for a long time.
A fear so strong that we did not even notice the moment
when a wish to climb a tree
overpowered the fear
of the government officials, who in their helplessness
and fear of heights, swayed the poplar
to silence the voice which so clearly described us.
Perhaps my neighbour was the only one who understood that the
        poplar was older
than the Presidential Palace.
Perhaps.

## CURTAINS

I wake you up in the middle of the night and say:
I'm having an interesting dream. Let's dream it together.
You just smile and turn onto your other side.
I just want to tell you
that on the corner of our bed,
our untouchable state with a sheet for a flag,
an Aboriginal and a Laplander sit
and leaf through a book on Indians.
I want to tell you
that our blanket resembles more and more the thick curtains
I drew over the windows to separate us from the street.
I want to tell you that for years now
I have been unable to sleep
watching you smile in yours.

## VICTORY

I was passing through a country which had won
the World Cup that same day. Crowds cried
*Victory, victory…*, running deliriously, state flags
fluttering behind them. It was a sight too rich
for my poor eyes. Only when the crowds
dispersed did I notice that someone had stolen
my bag of food.

Long ago, shooting a Russian submachine gun,
my father entered our town to celebrate another
victory with people who could only raise
flowers that year. "Victory, victory…" cried my
father, thin as death, adorned with flowers which
smelled of gunpowder.

For patriotic reasons he never went abroad and
the graveyard fence is the only border he will
ever cross.

That is why I don't like to meet him when he
returns from the market with an empty bag. *I did
not fight for this, they are swindling poor people*, he
shouts from the corridor. Mother drags him into
the kitchen and pours him a brandy. And I, like a
culprit, slip away from the house lest I ask myself
aloud: *Is this the same man I see in the photograph
entering the town and crying words which mean
nothing anymore?*

SPRING IS COMING

Spring is coming on crutches.
Swallows nest again in the ruins
and childrens' diapers flutter merrily on a clothesline
stretched between two graveyards. Peace
caught us unprepared to admit without shame
that we survived and that we dream about seagulls and the sea.
It brought restlessness to our Sunday suits and dancing shoes;
it settled in our stomachs like a disease.

Spring is coming on crutches.
Look, idle soldiers drunkenly roam the town
afraid they'll have to turn in their uniforms if they return home.
Look, they are carrying out a young man from the cinema
because he couldn't bear the beauty of a happy ending.
Look, the former hundred metre dash champion
sits alone at the stadium watching the shadow
of his wheelchair.
Even my neighbours don't quarrel with the same zeal
with which they were once nasty to one another.
It feels as if we woke up in our underwear under a spotlight
on the theatre stage, and we have yet to find the exit.
The peace halved us.

Spring is coming. On crutches.
The time of medals is coming,
when children from freshly whitewashed orphanages start
        searching for family albums,
the time when big flags cover this landscape of horror
in which my neighbour, in the basement,
holds a child's winter glove in his hand. And weeps.

## REPEATING IMAGES

A fly walks on the TV screen where the President
announces the terrible days to follow. Behind him is a flag.
Across from that flag, a woman counts change
from the sale of the morning paper.
Her son, hands dirty with printer's ink, sleeps.
Above his head is a picture clipped from the papers
in which the President shakes hands with the boy.
It is obvious that the boy is ashamed of his dirty hands.

A few kilometres further
a driver who was once the star student at his university
takes out a sandwich wrapped in yesterday's newspaper.
Behind him a dredge loads earth onto his truck.
He wonders:
How many anthems were sung for this earth, which
stirs up dust on my bullet-drilled truck?
How many tears were shed for this simple earth
before it swallowed the last generation of fighters
and became dust?

He unwraps yesterday's newspaper
and notices how sandwiches get smaller every day
and how love passes slowly, like the wind
which blows through the broken windshield
and carries away the fresh morning newspapers
he hasn't yet managed to read.

WHAT IS LEFT

What is left of our rebellion, which was not
mentioned in the daily papers? What is left of
our motives, remembered now only by a few
of us and by those we opposed?

Just a few torn posters, the smell of ink and
shame. The colours on our flags have faded, and
we now drag along dogs and children. Only the
street is still there. The sparrows still chirp, the
same ones which flew away the moment we
arrived glowing with change.

What is left of our conspiratorial candles, which
burned so fast we couldn't count ourselves?
Nothing but the glow of nervous cigarettes,
comets diving into ashtrays; nothing but
gunpowder voices, echoing first grade history.
Is that all?

If each new year didn't arrive with nice cakes
and end up with dirty plates, I would think that
I'd only imagined it all, that I'd protected myself,
sparrows as witnesses, from the emptiness which
makes me watch the street, and the boy who
throws a lighted firecracker into the snow.
Under my window.

*with* SORROW

## CANDLE OF THE NORTH

Take me to the beach, my darling,
let us walk over pebbles that don't smell of fish from the market,
walk where a breeze lazily leafs through last year's newspapers,
through decomposed documents of long-dead blood donors.

Take me to the beach
and keep in mind that I'm scared
watching children and emigrants cross the unlighted street.
I no longer care to hide in my pocket
fingers red with the pain
of turning the radio dial all night,
looking for a program that plays silence.
I am not ashamed of trying to think nothing, absolutely nothing.

Perhaps we might still see that hole in the sky from which
I cut out a whole constellation and gave it to you,
believing it would fit in your wallet.
Last Sunday I found the same stars in the basement
hiding amongst last year's horoscopes and newspaper clippings
about lucky lottery winners.

Take me to the beach
and walk with me over crossword-puzzle magazines
and let us listen to those crying children who are not my own
and let me just smile to people
who smile like me.

My hands are as cold as TV news, my skin as blue
as the stamp on a birth certificate.

But somewhere in a northern room
a strange candle burns and wakes me up,
a candle that I melt down,
and I smell soil when diving in my dream
to the bottom of the ocean,

looking for something that was promised to me
when I was born.

My hunting gun hangs on the wall
next to the photo of the deer
I followed into the minefield.
Every time I dream I walk to the stars
I find socks full of blood in the morning.

I know that East is easy,
that West is always opposite
and in the North lost people
sit around a single candle
to warm their cold fingers.
It is where mothers make sandwiches
already eaten by sorrow and the long wait
for better days to come.

For years I couldn't wash the breadcrumbs from my hands.
Were these crumbs from the school bags of northern children?
Those same children who need to recognize when they go home
the difference between streetlights and a wolf's shining eyes?

They are not breadcrumbs, I console myself,
they are just the black sand falling from that place
from which I cut the constellation.
But I know this is not the truth.
I once tattooed a lamb on my forehead
but when I woke the next day it had disappeared
and only bones remained.

So take me to the beach, my darling,
where every single pebble has its own rhyme,
nothing but a rhyme, with no meaning.

## THE ARRIVAL OF THE WOLF

Welcome wolf, among our bloodthirsty sheep,
all smiling at you just to show their teeth. Do not
be confused by the greasy dishtowels you see in
place of flags. Many conquerors have passed
through this city, and none has yet succeeded in
leaving his mark.

This is the time of chaos, and roses smell of skin.
It is so dark in the corridors you creep along and
the marble has eyes clearer than your own; it will
see beautiful women collecting your hairs for their
albums. Your gums gleam like medals at
celebrations, but the mirror does not tell you that
you no longer follow the deer spoor you've
sniffed through the herbarium of this city under
decaying stars.

Welcome wolf, with those funny jaws. Our
bloodthirsty sheep smile at you from the windows,
for you are not the wolf we fear. You are but a
shadow of the wolf that is following you.

Someone winds the clock after you arrive, and
wakens the moment you fall asleep, hurrying to
seal up the windows through which you could see
the forest. Mice will eat your documents because
they are not afraid of anything. They do not care
about the draft at your door, nor about the
shadow of the murderer above your bed.

These are turbulent times, and you are but a wolf
from a textbook, a stuffed fur on the wall of a
hunting lodge, in this town whose people no
longer resemble those of other towns you have
passed through.

## THE FIRST WAR VICTIM

The first victim was my desk. A bullet from who knows where went through my attic apartment's window and destroyed it, before disappearing, exhausted, into the bookshelves. I never found that bullet. Perhaps it lodged in one of the comic books I haven't read since then.

Not long after, I saw a film on TV about the Russian writer Limonov shooting from a hill with an anti-aircraft gun. I could have sworn he was shooting in my direction. I tore off the title page of his novel, and stuck it over the hole in my window. It is still there.

The war has been over for a long time. Instead of marching, former heroes with holes in their hearts walk the streets. No one wants to listen to their war stories anymore. When I was leaving my city for good I took with me just one book, the book with the missing cover.

Every letter I later sent to my old address I wrote on someone else's desk. I am a writer with a hole in his stomach.

Recently I got a letter from an old neighbour. She complained that the wind sometimes whistles so hard through the hole in the window that it sounds like a wounded soldier's moaning. "Anyway," she writes, "the book's cover is so faded no one can recognize the author's name or the title of the novel."

"What was the author's name, what was the name of the novel?" I'll soon start asking myself. Whenever I sit at a desk the same thoughts attack me: a character from a comic book fights the cobwebs and dust in my empty apartment. He is shot with a bullet from an anti-aircraft gun, a real bullet. And he screams and sounds like the wind which blows through the bullet hole in the window.

## A SHORT LECTURE ON LIFE

My father enters the room crying, the newspaper with my
    obituary notice
at the top of the page clenched in his hands. I can
                see my face.
You shouldn't have done this to me, he says, you should have
told me earlier. My pension is too low
and is good only for life.
That's not me, I tell him, it's probably some mistake.
Look how my hand turns the pages of this book,
listen to this pencil creak in my hand.
Listen to how alive I am.

It means nothing to me, he says. That paper you use
                to inform me
that you are alive is the same as the paper informing me
you are dead.
But I *am* alive, I tell him, can't you hear my voice
              talking to you
right now? Can't you hear me?
Forget that, he tells me, I imagined your voice earlier
and I've heard these very words many times before.
I watch him wipe his tears while walking down the stairs.
After all, I shout, I am quite sure I am alive,
I have all of the right documents with all of the official stamps.
              Listen to me!
Don't you shout at me, he says. You don't know a thing about life,
you don't know a thing about documents,
you have no right to speak about facts.
Then I hear the stairs creak under his feet,
I hear him cry quietly.

## ADAM

My name is Adam. They call me a boy.
They tell me I'll be grown when I fit
grandpa's shoes and can recognize the difference
between my sister's pubic hair and my own.
My grandpa was buried in his shoes long ago
and my sister locks the door
whenever she's in the bathroom. Through the keyhole
I have watched her take off her clothes
and caress her pointy breasts.
I read her diary and know for whom
she puts on lipstick. She will leave me soon
and nothing will remain with which to compare.

I know only that I was a boy just yesterday.
I'm the ghost of the house today,
growing up languid as a hothouse flower,
or a lizard daydreaming of becoming a dragon.

I know why my father grabs his gun
and runs up to the roof whenever the red
police light shines through my aquarium.
He never notices that I have emptied the bullets from his gun
and I never told him I couldn't stand
the thought of him in jail for years.

I know why my mother leaves at midnight,
picked up by a driver in a black limousine.
If I told her I used her needle to prick holes in her condoms
she still wouldn't understand how much I need her at home.

They chose the wrong uniform, my grandma tells me,
when they occasionally met and fought.
Before I grow up she'll awake and rise to the radio,
the same voice on the news promising the end of the war.
Now she listens to the fairy tales I read her every night

and looks happy. I never told her that the last rent packet we paid
held the shape of her wedding ring.
She's going to leave me soon, I know it
by the way she listens to my fairy tales, asking me
to avoid the parts when flowers die.

My name is Adam and I'm still a boy.
If I go to the movies I sit next to the exit
because some man always tells me
I shouldn't listen to my teachers
when they talk about love between boys and girls.

I didn't go back to school after a teacher
pushed me into the swimming pool.
I stayed underwater until he
had a heart attack.

Outside my window sad people walk the street
and compare themselves with passers-by.
Outside people wear masks while walking dogs.
Even dogs wear masks. Outside is a mess.

Sometimes I sit in the bathroom for hours
and imagine having a shower.

They say it happens to everybody.
But it happens now only to me.
To Adam, to the boy who sits in a cage,
believing invisible bars on his eyelids
protect him from the mess
outside his window.

## AN EXCERPT FROM MY CONVERSATION WITH GOD

I quarreled with god all night. What a nightmare.
I almost burst into tears when I realized that we resembled
a married couple divorcing because of adultery
even though still in love.
Absent-minded, with the north reflected in his eyes,
he listened to the war in my voice,
to my hundreds of questions which rang like answers.
He fidgeted, scratched behind his ear, coughed,
twisted his moustache, glanced at the ceiling,
and didn't say a thing.

I showed him the circle on the finger of an old woman
who had just sold her wedding ring.
I showed him a shoe thrown onto a garbage heap.
Is it the same shoe the boy with the crutches wears,
the one who is begging behind the church to buy back his
    family's history?
I think I told him even shaking hands would not
persuade me that he existed. But I'm not sure.

I woke up beside an ashtray full of cigarette butts
and felt better when the hangover hit.
I think I even smiled,
like a husband who after having agreed with his unfaithful wife
on all of the details of their divorce,
damages the elevator
and walks down from the hundredth floor,
stair by stair
impatient to recognize the one
who walks up.

ANGELS

Angels hover over this city that eats its own roads,
whose people disappear on trains. Can you hear them?
They are not the angels we remember from Christmas cards,
they don't resemble sleepy children anymore.
We live in a time of change
and everyone wears a blood-proof watch.

I am talking about angels who feel at home in police files,
about angels shaped like flies, buzzing around computers.
I swear I caught one trying to rip out my passport photo.
Another rewrote the prescription for my glasses.
I wonder less and less about the difference
between what I remember and what I see,
why I so often find feathers in my wallet
and holes in my pockets.

Angels hover and stardust falls from their wings and covers
bed frames made from Santa's sleigh,
pajamas that smell of graveyard soil.
They bribe the morning light to look like the TV screen
and our heads become so heavy
we understand nothing but weather reports.

They no longer live among the bright clouds
and don't waste time coaxing the wind to lift
schoolgirls' skirts for fun
or decorate trees with the hats of passers-by.
No more does Cupid sport with arrows and broken hearts,
no more are yesterday's lovers today's parents.
Angels now live among the greasy clouds,
counting tardy workers and their broken dreams.
They are too busy designing uniforms
to notice the boot prints of the soldiers that remain behind.

Who knows whether a postman will recognize our fear
when he comes near our famished mailbox?
Who knows whether a policeman on night shift
will recognize the sorrow tattooed on our hands
while waving to a flock of geese leaving town?
Will a lumberjack ever understand our tears
when he cuts down the apple tree that long produced
nothing but flowers?

Yes, angels hover over the city,
disguised in the white coats of doctors
who hide their nicotined fingers, and we resemble more and more
retired firefighters wandering in new uniforms.

Their fingers kiss our skin the way spiders
kiss the strings of the guitar we left in the basement
and never learned to play. Can you hear them laughing
while writing their names on the letters we send ourselves?

On the library shelves there are no more books about angels.
There is only a big hole through which one can hear screams
and smell the smoke of burning houses. We don't talk anymore.
We just whisper, wait for our children to come back from school
with notebooks full of writing about gentle angels
and their home among the bright clouds.

This is the year of change, we whisper and smile.
We whispered and smiled about changes last year too.

## DREAM NUANCE

I am blind, I say. Then I am silent for a long time. I lie.
I look out the window: freezing children sing
under the Christmas tree and the snow is like a rainbow.
Frozen sparrows fall from the branches onto a butcher
dragging a slaughtered lamb. It is night.
A picture of a saint blazes in the stove. The airports drone
and I feel like crying. I am blind, I say, I am blind.
She is silent, absent-mindedly taps her fingers on the table.

I've forgotten, I whisper. Then I'm dully silent. I lie.
In my X-ray eyes still sparkle three shoes cast
by a horse that fled long ago. I remember well:
with a chained dog father hunted men and I
barked at birds. Hotel vacuum cleaners now roar.
It is as dark as before and the air already smells of TV sets.
*Frost. Frost. Frost*, I repeat.
She keeps silent, as if she hasn't heard me at all.

And so I sit silent. After all, what else can I do? What?
I am already used to traffic lights, to the skin of a chameleon,
to someone who isn't me. It's cold. The universe buzzes
above the control tower, the fish serenely chew
oxygen bubbles, the orchards smell of hay. And it is dark.
Only now and then, someone from the bottle smiles as if
everything is just a dream nuance.
Can you see me? I ask her. Can you see me at all?
                              She nods. But she is lying.
I don't care anymore. She doesn't understand me anyway.

## BACK DOOR

While I watch the front door, officers with gold
buttons for eyes enter my back door and look for
my glasses. Their gloves leave the prints of their
ranks on the plates in which I find my reflection,
on the cups from which I never drink, on the
windows bending outward. Then they leave
with crude jokes about the women I once loved.

Through my back door the police enter
regularly, with rubber pencils behind their belts.
Like kisses their ears splash when they stick to
my books which whine at night like pet dogs in
the snow. Their fingerprints remain on my
doorknob when they leave through my back
door, and their uniforms fade like cans in the
river.

Why do postmen enter through my back door
with bags stinking of formalin? Their heavy
soldier boots march through my bathroom and I
can hear them looking for the pajamas hidden in
a box of carbon paper. I ask them why they need
my pajamas and their eyes flash for a moment
with April tenderness. Then they slam the door
and the room is illumined by darkness.

And I still watch the front door where the
shadow of someone's hand lies by the doorbell.
Someone should enter. Someone should enter
soon.

## STORMY NIGHT

It's a stormy night in Bosnia. There's nothing on TV, not yet,
until some drunken soldier eats his frozen medals. Then I guess
even the swollen leaves in his pockets will be a kind of news. I bet
then we'll even pay attention to the neighbour's cat. O yes

we're all only last year's story, people who really died last Fall
but don't know it yet. The old calendar just lost the old year
but even he toothlessly smiles, already married to my wall.
My summer shoes walked off to the pawn shop. And I fear

someone will buy them, thinking they're wings made of leather.
Yes, they are different sizes but they shine like a spring sun.
Whoever buys them will be wrong, thinking that a goose feather
will lead him to the nest. But they will never fly or run

if the buyer has no home. Shoes are just shoes. They bribe
with the smell of soil and the promise of tight laces.
A soldier watches them, he's got the day off from his tribe
of dead soldiers who just arrived with no guns and no faces.

O God, please don't let him buy them. If he walks away
        with my shoes
death will be the pawnbroker who takes my Spring for a
        bottle of booze.

## WINTER THAT LASTS IN THE SKIN OF WOMEN

Slowly, the snow melts.
I do not know who I am. But I know
women will give birth to pregnant daughters,
that they will plant the trees that are a forest
from the moment they sob together,
not knowing for whom.
With an axe hung from his belt, someone will stand
above beds covered by last season's leaves
and so the past will be renewed.
And I will try to guess who it is, and whether or not he looks like me
even though I have only seen my blood in a test tube.

The snow melts.
The creek bears my mother's hair ribbons,
my sister's diary and the dog collar I wore
until I learned how to bark and hide the cat's heart
beneath my black fur. If I stayed longer I would probably
see the leaves I collected for my herbarium long ago
before learning from melting icicles
that grass smells only when it's cut,
that in my temple of bones
I breathe only swaths while comparing the claws
and nails of my hundred fingers.
So I've grown.

O tell me who I am.
For a long time I lived with my literary imagination.
For a long time now I have hovered over a bookshelf,
an inkless page. Too many things remind me of death,
of this planet I dare not touch.

Watching the shadow of someone with an axe in his belt
I doubt more and more.
Yes, I doubt more and more often
that the snow melts at all.

## I WAS A FOOL

I was a fool to guard my family house in vain
watching over the hill somebody else's house shine,
and, screaming, die in flames. I felt no sorrow and no pain
until I saw the torches coming. The next house will be mine.

If I wasn't somebody else, as all my life I've been,
I wouldn't say to my neighbour that I feel perfectly fine
upon seeing his beaten body. I should offer my own skin
as a tarp. Will the next beaten body be mine?

I was a fool. I love this sentence. Long live Goran and his sin.
There is no house or beaten man. There is no poetry, no line,
there is no war, there are no neighbours. There's no tarp made of skin.
But there's a pain in my stomach as I write this. It's only mine,

this sentence, the one I swallowed, whose every word
is each of the flames I saw, every scream a sword.

## MY SHADOW

Her fingers were in my pocket.
She checked the government stamp on my ID,
the stamp across my smiling face,
though I no longer remember what I was smiling for.
I only remember that the shoes
I didn't try were pinching me.

She breathes under my pillow,
caresses the rabbit-fur cover of my passport.
Her breath smells of ashes,
her touch soft on my skin.
She smells everything, even my suit
on the other half of the bed
still littered with crumbs from a wedding cake.
She knows everything. The house knows her fingertips.

She has slept in my work clothes.
She has silenced my alarm clock.

Because of her I dream of darkness,
which spreads like an illness over my body.
Because of her I chew on horror
the way a shell chews its pearl.

Who will eat my breakfast tomorrow morning?
Who will tell my boss I will be late again?
Who will listen to my fellow workers make jokes?
A shadow is a poor excuse.

They know nothing about my shadow.
They know nothing about how day follows day
and I no longer recognize my face in the mirror.
They do not know my shadow shaves every morning.
And how every morning I would cut my skin
if I wasn't afraid I might see
no blood.

## CLIMBING UP AGAIN

Where are my friends, I ask you? Where are they?
I shout on the stairway while the wind whistles
through the broken panes of the entry.
Tell me and I'll protect you with this uniform
made from my skin,
yes, me, the man with a graphite voice
and an eraser's soul.

Can you hear
the breath of the lovers who left their
chalky names in the corridors,
the shadows that giggle in the empty mailbox,
all part of that everyday ritual that protects us
from one another?
I am measured by the one who breathes most loudly,
as are you.

Don't let this miner's lamp confuse you,
the one that falls from my hand and rolls down the stairway
when I show you my dog's photograph.
There, I tell you,
greasy clouds whisper above the television aerials
and persuade you to switch them on.
Convicts selling small crucifixes knock on your door
to sell you on the beauty of death,
though you don't see it.
You listen with fear and think that I am wrong
when I claim that every day dawns dark,
from soldiers' boots thudding steps of unclear origin.

I miss my friends, I whisper to you.
Do not fear my glance above the elevator's alarm.
I console myself by carrying bullet cases
which remind me that I could have been someone else.

I've practiced life too long, I tell you.
I like only your ears,
which try to defend themselves while I explain
that I am climbing the stairs with a night shift of miners.

I hear the needle and thread in your sleeve,
I sniff machine oil, I feel the tailor's sweat
when I ask you to show me the way to the hill
where I was born as a bird
a long time before I learned to crawl.

Perhaps I will find my friends there,
my generation of corpses with whom I'll die
fighting for the same breath.

But you flee. I sink deeper. Deeper.
In the snow. Which remains. After you. While the wind whistles.
Through broken. Panes. Of the entry.

"A newborn baby's shirt should not be as white as a freshly painted house," said my grandfather Vaso. "If we are talking about a boy, his sleeves should be dirty. Men's hands are made of soil. If it is a girl, until she is old enough to understand that gold suits her better, there should be a stain on her neck from a necklace made of clay. In any case, don't forget to give a baby boy a watch.

"A bride's wedding dress should not be as white as the walls of the apartment she will live in," said my grandfather Vaso. "It should be sprayed with wine from her father's lips, her mother's tears. The bridegroom's shirt should not be so white that guests notice the dirty rings from his hands made of soil. Naturally, the newlyweds will not care because they will be transfixed by the reflection of their faces in their gold wedding rings. Only later will they understand the importance of these things.

"A woman's funeral dress shouldn't always be black. It should have the soft buttons of candle wax drops, like the eyes of a dying person. Like the front of a house riddled by bullets from a rifle on the day a first child is born. Men's shirts should always be sweaty."

My grandfather told me this while putting on a clean, white shirt. He lay down on the bed, ready to die.

"I didn't expect you to die in a clean, white shirt," I told him. He removed his watch from his wrist. He got it the day he was born.

"I count on your tears," he said. Then he died. He never did answer my question how it was that he could always tell the right time, even though his watch never worked.

## TRANSISTOR RADIO

In my entire life I was never so ashamed of
myself as I was that summer in 1995, lying on a
quiet Italian beach, playing with my children in
the sand, far from snipers and the besieged city.
Far from danger. At a certain point, upset from
trying without success to find some Bosnian
radio station with news about the war, I threw
my little transistor radio into the sea. No news
means no more bad news, I told myself, and
turned my attention to the drawings my
children were doing in the sand. My daughter
had just made a butterfly, my son struggled to
shape a bird.

Suddenly a little wet gypsy boy showed up with
the sea soaked radio and told me that everything
would be okay if I let it dry and bought new
batteries. I watched that little boy, who was
already running back to the sea, wanting to ask
him how many radios he'd already saved from
the dark waters. I wanted him to tell me that I
was not the only sad man asking himself: who
am I to have survived? How many of us have
thrown radios into the sea, only to wait for the
night to go secretly, as I did, and buy new
batteries? But he was gone, and I couldn't
remember the language he'd spoken. The only
trace he left were footprints on my daughter's
butterfly and my son's bird.

War is the beast that lives on a dusty television screen.
The TV's off. There is no war. It happens now to others.
My mother is a burnt house. Her ghost was last seen
cursing a lot of soldiers and the few remaining fathers.

Dad is late again. He knows where I am, I guess.
Maybe he missed the train. He'll surely catch another.
I hug myself like a pillow. I love myself less
now that I'm my own goodnight kiss, my own goodnight mother.

But tomorrow's Sunday. The TV will be off. Let it pass.
The soldier's grave receives a child's blessing.
TV Guide, Your Majesty, please don't let anyone ask:
What are you watching? Is your father still missing?

## OLD PEOPLE TRAVEL NORTH
## (POST WAR POEM)

We are driving north, Chelsea and I. We sold
the house, we gave to our neighbours the things
we didn't need anymore and then spat out the
window as we left the city. Our fingers are still
sticky from the goodbye cake. We are now
driving through the desolate prairie. God
obviously isn't interested in living here.

"Look at all the raccoons killed on the road,"
I say to Chelsea, "what's so magical on the other
side? What attracts them so much that they
ignore the roaring cars and glaring lights?"

"I'm glad we never had children," Chelsea says,
and closes her eyes.

I watch her falling into sleep. I notice the
moment she crosses the line. Behind that line
are blooming fields, maybe children happily
playing on the porch. Maybe she goes to live in
another house and celebrates Christmas with
somebody who is not me. Just like that, she
leaves me alone with my questions and my sticky
fingers on the steering wheel. She never did
anything like that before.

Please don't die here and now on the road,
I beg you, don't die the same way those careless
raccoons did, running to something promising
on the other side. In just a few hours we will be
at the door of our Nursing Home. Smiling
nurses await us. Blooming roses on the table of
our small room wait for us.

A kind attendant will take our suitcases to our room. They are light because the only thing we took with us were doctor's prescriptions and receipts from the funeral home proving that we already paid for our deaths. Soon the nursing home manager will come with a bottle of watery champagne to welcome us.

We will have a couple of hours to hang up the pictures of the pets we gave to the neighbours. After that we will be ready to relax, enjoy the sunset as the dying sun warms the coffins in our hearts.

But you don't wake up. With my hands on the wheel, I feel the need to drive over the raccoons' dead bodies. Trying to wake you up.

# ACKNOWLEDGEMENTS

SOME OF THESE POEMS have been published in different collections in England, Finland, Poland, Norway, Sweden, Holland, Denmark, Bosnia-Herzegovina, Slovenia, and Serbia, and have been translated into more than ten languages. Some were also included in anthologies of world poetry such as *Scanning the Century* (Penguin), *101 Poems Against War* (Faber&Faber), and *Banned Poetry* (Index).

Some of these poems have also been used in the films *I do not Dream in English* (Finland), *Burning Books* (Norway), and *Rewind Tape* (Denmark). Some have also been set as part of the libretto for the opera *Sarajevo*, by Scottish composer Nigel Osborne.

Sixteen of the poems in this collection I either wrote in English or translated into English myself. I did this partly out of my need to see how comfortable I could be in a language I was not born with, and partly so that I wouldn't feel like a stranger in this country where I've lived since leaving that country of my birth. If the reader doesn't recognize a big difference between Amela's and my own translations, then I will consider it as a compliment to both of us.

New wars replace old wars. The horror fades, especially when it happens to others. I imagined this collection as a testament as much as it is a celebration of poetry.

Special thanks to Visnja for her support. Many thanks to Amela Simić for her translations, my editors Dan and Sal, the poet Fraser Sutherland and the playwright Sang Kim. Thank you Susan Sontag, wherever you are now. It is probably the same place as Simon from Nantes, who brought me three bags of flour and committed suicide in order to forget the horror.

Thank you Saba, my beautiful dog, for teaching my children how to walk before you wandered into a minefield. Thank you Hillary Weston for breaking my back during the years I worked as a simple labourer in your Toronto based Holt Renfrew warehouse. I survived as a poet.

This book is for my mother Rŭza, who decided not to survive another war, and for my brother Stojan, who didn't survive the sniper's bullet through his heart.

## ABOUT THE POET

**Goran Simić** was born in Bosnia in 1952 and has lived
in Toronto since 1996. He has published eleven books
of poetry, drama, and short fiction. In Canada, Simić
has published *Immigrant Blues* (Brick Books, 2003) and
*Peace and War*, a limited edition collection of his poems
and those of Fraser Sutherland. His poetry and drama
have been translated into more than ten languages. His
poems have also appeared in anthologies of world po-
etry such as *Banned Poetry* (Index, 1997) and *Scanning
the Century* (Penguin, 2002).

# ABOUT THE TRANSLATOR

**Amela Simić** is a translator and writer. Her translations from English of works by Susan Sontag, Bernard Malamud, Sylvia Plath, Joyce Carol Oates, Joseph Heller, Saul Bellow, Michael Ondaatje, and Lawrence Durrell, among others, have appeared in various literary magazines of the former Yugoslavia. She has also translated several novels, and works by contemporary philosophers. Her essays and translations of Bosnian poetry have appeared in *Salmagundi*, *TLS*, *The Paris Review*, *Canadian Forum*, *Meta*, and *BBC Radio*. She is currently the Executive Director of Playwrights Guild of Canada and lives in Toronto.

Typeset in Bembo by Dennis Priebe,
*from Sarajevo, with Sorrow* was printed offset on Strathmore
Laid and Smyth-sewn at Gaspereau Press in an edition of
500 copies. The jacket was printed letterpress on a
Vandercook 219 from photopolymer plates. An additional
25 copies were case bound by Daniel Wells.

BIBLIOASIS
WINDSOR, ONTARIO, CANADA